TO SPRING WITH LOVE

Seasons of Summer Novella Series: Book Three

MELISSA BALDWIN

ISBN: 0692916431
ISBN 13: 978-0692916438

About To Spring With Love

I, Summer Peters, am thrilled to be done with the frigid winter. Spring is in the air, and I'm ready for a fresh new start. My career is flourishing, I'm searching for a new place to live, and I'm finally ready to take my relationship with Alexander Williams to the next level.

Unfortunately, Alexander's assistant, Melanie, seems to be up to her old tricks, even stooping as low as dating my ex-boyfriend, Jake. And I constantly feel like I'm facing a dilemma of having to share Alexander with a woman who's out to destroy our relationship.

To add to these challenges, I receive devastating news from my best friend, Angie. I'm saddened to learn she may not be here when I need her the most. I'm realizing that I may need to lean on someone I never expected during this time of change.

Continue to follow Summer on her wild one-year journey in this third book of the Seasons of Summer Novella Series from USA Today bestselling author Melissa Baldwin.

I dedicate this book to you, the person reading this. Thank you for your support and for taking time out of your life to read my stories. I hope this book brings a smile to your face and makes you laugh out loud. Stay tuned for more fun coming your way!

*a*h . . . I have really missed the sun. I absolutely love when spring comes, especially being able to sit outside and not worry about my toes falling off from frostbite. I probably should move to a warmer climate but my life is here in Connecticut. Speaking of moving, I'm finally looking at a few new places this afternoon.

I've been so busy with my company, Summer Interiors, that my moving plans have fallen by the wayside, and I'm sure my landlord, Mrs. Rothera, is happy about this. I think she actually likes having me there. It's not that I don't like where I live, I do. But with my apartment comes a reminder of my former relationship and a landlord who likes to give unsolicited advice. Let's just say it seems a little crowded (and I'm not talking about the space).

My friend Angie thinks I'm subconsciously waiting for one of two things to happen, either an invitation to move in with my boyfriend or a marriage proposal. She tends to be slightly overdramatic because I doubt either of these will happen any time soon.

Don't get me wrong, I would love to live in my boyfriend's house because it's exactly what I picture my dream house would be. I still think both of those options may be a bit premature, even though we've both come a long way. When we got together last fall, we were both recently out of relationships, so we decided to take things slow. I was especially cautious because my heart was broken and my breakup was one-sided, and it wasn't my side.

I'm still so cautious that I still haven't said the L word, even after he blurted it out after a tumultuous Valentine's date. Alexander, being the amazing guy he is, says that he's patient and will wait until I'm ready. I know I have very strong feelings for him, but for some reason, I still can't bring myself to admit these yet.

"Let's do this," Angie says cheerfully, interrupting my daydream. She seems to be in a great mood. Not that I blame her, after months of frigid winter the mild temperatures are having a great impact on everyone.

"We'll go soon," I tell her. "Just have a seat for a few minutes and enjoy the sunshine." I'm expecting a lecture from her on my levels of procrastination, but she surprises me when she sits down and orders a latte.

"So, I have some news," she yells. Angie talks really loudly, so it always seems like she's yelling even when she's not. "I think Brett's going to propose to me."

My mouth drops open. "What? How do you know?"

"Well, I don't exactly, but Mrs. Rothera says something big is about to happen, and Brett has been acting funny. He says he's planning a surprise trip for us."

I shake my head. "Why don't you let him surprise you? Don't ruin it for him."

She rolls her eyes. "I'm not ruining anything, and you know I hate surprises."

I lean over and give her a hug. "This is so exciting. When's the trip?"

Angie's smile starts to fade. "What's she doing here? Is she following you now?"

"Who?" I turn around to see whom she's looking at. Sure enough, it's Alexander's assistant, Melanie, aka my archnemesis, sitting at a table by herself.

I groan and turn back around in my chair. I even put my sunglasses on in hopes that she doesn't recognize me. "I doubt she's following me. I actually haven't seen her in a while since Alexander practically banished her from his house. I'm sure she has a voodoo doll with my name on it, though."

Angie starts to giggle. "Probably. Maybe we should invite her to join us."

I snort. "Um, that's definitely not happening. I'm not spending this beautiful day with that . . ."

"No freaking way," Angie interrupts me. She has an absolutely horrified look on her face.

"What now?" I exclaim.

I spin around again, but this time I see that Melanie is no longer by herself. Someone has joined her and that someone just happens to be my ex-boyfriend, Jake. The same ex-boyfriend who blindsided me by ending our relationship last summer.

"Do they know each other?" she asks in a loud whisper. At least she isn't yelling across the café anymore.

My mind wanders back to Valentine's night on a cold New York City street when Melanie walked outside to find me in Jake's arms. It was completely innocent as he was trying to comfort me. I thought she was going to run to Alexander and make a scene, but it didn't go down that way. I remember running down the street to clear my head, leaving Jake and Melanie standing alone.

"I think they do," I reply absently.

"Do you think she's up to something?" Angie asks.

I take a long sip of my coffee. "I don't know, but I'm going to find out."

Angie folds her arms and stares me down. It almost feels like she's my mother and she's waiting for me to crack and admit I've done something bad. Like that time in high school when I snuck out of my window in the middle of the night to go watch movies at my friend's house.

I admit I can't look her in the eye right now.

"Okay, Ang, why are you staring at me like that?" I ask defensively.

She breaks her dead stare long enough to sip her latte.

"Does that bother you?"

"Does what bother me?"

She rolls her eyes. "Seeing Jake with someone else."

Okay, maybe it does bother me a little, but I'm not sure if it bothers me that Jake is with another woman or the fact that the woman is Melanie. Melanie has made it her mission to cause issues in my relationship with Alexander. Up until recently, she's been in my face daily, and according to Alexander's ex-wife, this isn't new behavior for her.

"If you're implying that I'm jealous, I'm not," I snap.

"Calm down," she says, rolling her eyes.

I look over my shoulder once more and notice that Melanie is flirtatiously laughing. I've never heard her laugh like that before. Jake is smiling and clearly enjoying himself.

I scowl. I wonder if this is another ploy in her bag of tricks to drag me away from Alexander. Maybe she thinks I will get jealous and go back to Jake. He's told me on a few occasions that he has regrets about the way things ended between us. (The way *he* ended things.)

"I think it's time to go," I say quickly.

Angie nods, trying to hide her smile.

"Shut up," I say through my frustration.

We're able to escape the café without either Melanie or Jake seeing us, at least I don't think they saw us. When I looked back at them before leaving, they appeared to be pretty deep in their conversation. Honestly, if Jake keeps Melanie busy so she's out of my life, then that's better for me.

Next time I go apartment hunting, I'm going alone. Not that I mind having Angie with me but I think the pressure's getting to me. I'm not sure what it is I'm looking for in a new apartment, but I'm not having much luck. To add to my rising stress level, I certainly don't need Angie hanging over my shoulder suggesting I just ask Alexander if I can move in with him. Not even the topic of her possible engagement could distract her from Alexander and my dream home (aka his home).

When I finally get home, the last thing I want is a visit from my landlord. Of course, I'm in my apartment for approximately three minutes when I hear six familiar knocks on my door. (She always knocks six times.) I let out a loud sigh as I make my way to the door. I could totally lie and claim I was in the shower, but I know she wouldn't buy it. And of course, there's that whole psychic thing. She's for real, too, and I'm not talking about those TV commercials where they charge you eight dollars a minute for your phone call.

"I'm sorry to bother you," she says, as she pushes past me and walks into my apartment. She doesn't seem the least bit sorry. "I just had to show you these photos I found online. Since we've finished the living room and kitchen, I think I would like to go ahead with the bedrooms now instead of waiting."

I just finished decorating a few rooms in her apartment, and it wasn't an easy task. In fact, it was quite the opposite since she changed her mind more times than I can count. She said she wanted to hold off on the bedrooms, but I guess she's changed her mind already. Figures.

"I know I said I wanted to wait, but everything looks so new and fresh that I'm ready do it all."

I grit my teeth. The problem with Mrs. Rothera is that I don't know if I should try to pretend because I feel like she can see right through me.

"And since you will be moving out soon, I should take advantage of you living here for as long as I can," she adds.

I shrug my shoulders. "Maybe."

She gives me a curious look. "Is there a problem?"

I sit down at the table. "Not a problem exactly. I just haven't had any luck finding a place yet."

One corner of her mouth curls up, and it looks like she's smiling. She hasn't been happy about me moving out, which I can understand. I'm sure it can be stressful finding new tenants, and good ones for that matter.

"That's a shame. I'm sure you'll find something," she says unconvincingly.

She joins me at the table. "Can I ask what else has you so distracted?"

I hate to ask her for any kind of advice because she will take it and run. I've been very vocal that I have no desire to hear any details about my future. But, I don't think asking for advice is the same thing.

"My friend Angie says I should ask Alexander to move in with him." I pause. "Remember, I'm asking for your advice, not a reading. I'm not sure if it's too soon . . ."

"Much too soon," she interrupts. "It's best that you don't take that kind of a step so early in your relationship."

I nod. "Thank you. I agree."

She closes her eyes for a few seconds, and then opens them again. Her blank stare is kind of creeping me out.

"Anyway, I really need to get some work done. It's been a long day." I jump up from the chair and make my way toward the door. Thankfully, she follows me. "Make a list of some ideas for the bedrooms, and I will stop by later this week."

She pats me on the shoulder on her way out the door. "That would be wonderful."

Before I have a chance to close the door, she holds her arm out. "Oh, and don't forget you're welcome to stay here for as long as you need."

I force a smile and thank her before closing the door.

Chapter Two

I can't help but stare at Alexander's face. Seriously, my man is so gorgeous. I remember the first time I searched Alexander Williams online. And no, I'm not a crazy stalker; I was actually doing research before our first meeting. I admit I didn't expect him to be so attractive. I had a picture in my mind of a man, maybe mid-fifties, kind of a recluse who was looking to redecorate his drafty old house. Imagine how surprised I was to find out he was a mid-thirties, recently divorced man who just happened to look like Clark Kent, aka Superman.

Staring at him definitely helps to keep me from getting irritated that Melanie has already called him two times since we arrived at the restaurant. I have no doubt she knows he's with me.

"Tell him I will schedule a conference call in the morning," he says.

I swirl my wine around while I semi-patiently wait for him to finish his call.

He puts his phone down. "I'm sorry. We're in the middle of an acquisition, so everything is a bit more urgent."

Everything is urgent to Melanie, I think to myself.

"Tell me about the apartments you looked at. Was there anything good?"

I shake my head. "Unfortunately, no."

It's very possible I'm being extra picky when it comes to moving. Maybe this is a sign that I shouldn't move?

"I don't know. I'm starting to think I should just stay where I am for now."

Right at that moment, Alexander's phone rings again. He lets out an exasperated sigh.

"I'm not answering it," he insists.

Although I appreciate his gesture, I know he needs to answer it.

"It's okay," I tell him.

He grabs my hand and kisses it before picking up his phone. He doesn't let go of my hand.

"Yes, Melanie." He pauses. "That's perfect. Yes, schedule it."

As soon as he hangs up, I watch the phone intently, waiting for it to ring again.

"Melanie says she's sorry for all the phone calls and she will leave me alone for the rest of the evening."

Sure she is. All of a sudden, the image of her and Jake at the café flashes through my head.

"That reminds me, Angie and I saw Melanie at the café yesterday," I tell him.

He tears off a piece of a roll and puts it in his mouth.

"Really? How did that go? Any punches thrown?" he asks, raising an eyebrow.

I giggle. "No, but I don't think she saw us. She seemed . . . preoccupied."

He gives me a funny look. "What do you mean?"

I shift around in my chair. I immediately regret bringing this up.

"It's not a big deal. We were just surprised when we saw the person she was with."

"Who was it?" he asks curiously. Now I definitely have his attention.

I bit my lower lip. "I'm sure it's not a big deal, but she was with Jake."

He looks completely shocked. "Jake? You mean your ex-boyfriend, Jake?"

I nod. "Yeah. I remember seeing them talking at the restaurant opening and . . . anyway, I don't think they saw us. We left shortly after they arrived."

Alexander doesn't say anything. Perhaps this is the news he needed to hear to make him realize how much Melanie dislikes me? Why else would she be meeting with my ex-boyfriend?

"Do you think they're seeing each other?" he asks.

I shrug my shoulders. "I don't know. But it would be strange if they were, considering the situation." And by situation, I mean the fact that she's in love with Alexander and I'm the other woman. Not to mention Jake has been going out of his way to rectify what happened last summer.

He stares off into the distance. I probably shouldn't have said anything.

"Yes, it would be strange. Of course, I have no right to tell Melanie whom she can be involved with, but considering the history here, I don't think it's appropriate."

Hah! *Take that, Melanie.* Unfortunately, I can see how distracted Alexander is, and I only have myself to blame. I barely had his attention before, and now he's completely shut down.

"Can we just forget about them for the rest of the evening?" I plead.

Without saying a word, he leans over and kisses me. Our dinner date ends up being very nice, and shockingly, Melanie keeps her promise. There isn't one more phone call from her.

The only awkward moment of the night is when I mention Helena's apartment. Helena is Alexander's ex-wife; a few months ago, she asked me to redecorate her apartment. After I finally agreed, I visited her Tribeca apartment only to be met with a wall dedicated to memories of her life with Alexander. Following our meeting, I sent her the contract and she has yet to send it back to me. Both Angie and my friend Gina think she was playing me the whole time. They think she had no intention of hiring me and she used it as a way to make me jealous of her past with Alexander.

"Helena is known for her procrastination. The last time I saw her she told me she would be contacting you to finalize everything."

The truth is I don't want to decorate Helena's apartment. If I had my way, she would be completely out of our lives. Unfortunately, that's never going to happen since Alexander and Helena have the same best friends. She's part of the package whether I like it or not.

"It's fine. I've got plenty to keep me busy," I reply.

The subject of Helena is still a sensitive subject between us. After being reminded of their intense relationship and seeing them interact, I was almost ready to end my relationship with Alexander. This all happened at the opening of a restaurant I decorated. Needless to say, I may have overreacted slightly, but I can't help the way I feel.

"I have another referral for you," he says, changing the subject.

I place my hand on his cheek. My business has tripled since I decorated Alexander's house, and I know I owe it all to him. Another new client is just what I need since I'm sure I won't be doing business with Helena.

"That's awesome. Who?"

He smiles excitedly. "My parents."

His parents? Is it really time to meet the parents? I don't know why this freaks me out so much. I haven't thought about introducing my family to Alexander yet. And I'm sure they aren't ready either after the situation with Jake. Although, my father was quite pleased when Jake and I broke up. He never liked him anyway, and I'm still not sure why.

"Your parents need a decorator?"

He nods. "Yes. But, I'm actually the one hiring you. Their fiftieth wedding anniversary is coming up, and I would like to do it for them as a gift."

"So, it's a surprise?"

I don't have a good feeling about this. I would never go into someone's home and change things around without them being in agreement.

"Oh no, they know about it. So, if you're interested, they've invited us to dinner and you can sit down with my mom to discuss ideas. That is, if you want the job?"

This is his way of introducing me to his parents? This should make me feel more secure in our relationship, but for some reason, it doesn't.

"You're making that poor man wait? I would bet fifty bucks that you're the first woman to do that."

My friend Gina has no inner monologue.

"I just want to make sure the timing is right. We've had a lot of roadblocks in our way already."

She's leaning back in her chair with her feet up on the desk. "He's already told you he's in love with you, so why haven't you told him? You're going to give him a complex."

I roll my eyes.

"He knows I'm being cautious, and he's fine with that."

She's looking at her phone, so I'm not sure if she's still listening or if I've bored her already.

"Does this have anything to do with Jake?" she asks.

I look up from my laptop screen.

"Why would this have anything to do with Jake?"

She shrugs.

"Angie told me you guys saw him with Alexander's assistant. That girl never gives up, does she?"

Even though we all think she's using Jake to get to me, it's very possible that they're really seeing each other, and I can't do anything about it. Alexander certainly didn't like the idea, so I don't think I've heard the end of it. If anything, her being distracted is certainly better for my relationship.

"I don't know what's going on between them. I'm expecting Alexander to find out. He was not happy when I told them we saw them together."

Gina puts her feet down on the floor.

"Was he mad?"

"Not exactly mad, but he did say he thought it was inappropriate."

She purses her lips.

"Huh. Maybe he's jealous."

What does she mean by that?

I laugh. "Why would he be jealous that she was with Jake?"

She gives me a look that clearly says she thinks I'm being naïve. I've seen this look before.

"Not necessarily that she was with Jake, just that she was with another man in general."

Seriously? She thinks Alexander is jealous that Melanie was out with someone. I'm sure she has dated people in the time she's worked for him. Right?

"All I'm saying is that men can be very territorial over their employees, and even though he may not be interested in her in a romantic way, he may not want another man to step in and take her attention away from him. And let's be honest, I'm sure he likes the attention she gives him. I certainly wouldn't mind having someone at my beck and call every day."

As crazy as this sounds, she may be onto something here. Alexander is extremely dependent on Melanie, so much that he's kept her around even after she caused issues in his marriage.

"Well, I for one hope she finds someone else," I insist. "Then maybe she will get out of our lives."

Gina raises her eyebrows.

"Even if that someone is Jake?"

I scowl. "Yes."

Thankfully, Gina has an appointment, so we end this conversation. My mind starts to wander to Melanie and her romantic history. I wonder if she's dated anyone in the few years she's worked for Alexander. I know how completely devoted she is to him, so I'm guessing she hasn't. What are the chances she's finally found someone else and that someone just happens to be my ex-boyfriend? Ugh. This just gets more and more complicated.

Chapter Three

I love how it feels when I complete a project. There is such an overwhelming feeling of accomplishment, and I love when my clients are happy. I just finished decorating a home for the son of Brad Cooper. Mr. Cooper was one of the first clients Summer Interiors had, and he also happens to be Jake's boss. I was a little nervous when he contacted me about working on a second project with him, especially considering Jake and I are no longer together. Thankfully, the project was a huge success, and I can add another beautiful home to my portfolio.

Ever since I was a little girl I knew I wanted to be an interior decorator. I will never forget when my mom bought a Victorian floral couch for her formal living room. She let me help her pick out the color for the walls. We painted the room a very pale pink to bring out the pink tones in the couch. This was in the '80s of course. Some of my favorite memories are of visiting furniture stores and model homes to check out the décor. My brother and I would walk down the rows in the store and pretend we lived there.

The best part of my job is going into a building for the first time and seeing it as a blank canvas. So, why am I so nervous when Alexander sends me some pictures of his parents' home? The home is very nice, a little outdated but nothing too horrible. Of course, I want to make a good impression on his parents without suggesting they change things they may love about their home.

There's a knock at my door, and I glance at the time. It's a bit early for Mrs. Rothera, considering she tends to sleep in. She doesn't use alarms of any kind because she claims they disturb the natural rhythm of the body or something like that.

When I answer the door, I find Angie standing there, and I immediately notice that something is off. It's not unusual for her to show up at my door at this time of day, but today she's not herself.

"What's the matter?" I ask worriedly.

She holds up a tray of coffee cups and a box of donuts.

I raise my eyebrows as I hold the door open for her to come in. She puts everything on the coffee table and falls dramatically down on the couch.

"Are you planning on talking to me or should I guess why you look so devastated?"

She opens her coffee cup and dumps in a few creamers and sugar.

"Of course I'm going to talk, why else would I be here?" she wails.

Angie can be slightly overdramatic, so I sit next to her on the couch and open the donut box.

"We're moving," she blurts out.

I give her a curious look. "What? Who's moving?"

She hangs her head while playing with her coffee cup. "Brett and I are moving . . . to Florida."

I sit still for few seconds as I try to collect my thoughts. I let her words register in my brain, my best friend is moving . . . and to Florida?

"Hold on," I exclaim. "Why don't you start at the beginning?"

She reaches for a chocolate donut and takes a huge bite. After she devours the entire thing, she lets out a deep sigh.

"Remember when I told you that Mrs. Rothera said something big was happening. Well, I thought Brett was going to propose, so I finally asked him why he's been acting so strange. He says he was planning a trip to Orlando for us so he could tell me about the new job offer. He's asked me to go with him, and of course I said yes."

I must be in shock. Angie is moving to sunny, warm Florida. Also known as the home of Disney World, humidity, and alligators.

"Of course, I can run Friendship Travel from anywhere, so it's not that big of a deal for me. And just think, now you can come visit during the winter months and we can go to Disney World and the beach."

I nod slowly.

"Summer? Are you okay?"

I feel like crying. What am I going to do without my best friend?

"Yeah. When is this move happening?"

She frowns. "Within the next few months, he wants to find a house and get settled before the school year starts."

"I had no idea he was looking for a new job. Especially not thousands of miles away," I say softly.

She shrugs. "We've talked about it in the past, but I figured it would be a while." She stops and reaches for another donut.

I have to wonder if Angie is really happy about this. Yes, she can work her business from anywhere, but her life is here.

"Brett's dad is there and so are Isabella and Antonietta and their families. It's really a good move, and let's face it, this past winter was a killer."

I can't disagree with her about the winter, it was miserable. But I'm a little surprised she wants to live near her sisters. It's not that she doesn't get along with them, but they tend to be slightly overbearing.

"Wow." That's all I can say at this point.

"I know it's a shock, but it's going to be okay. And you have a terrific future ahead of you with Alexander."

I sigh as I take another donut out of the box. "I wish I was as confident about my relationship as you are."

She shakes her head. "Why do you say that? Does this have to do with Helena again?"

I shake my head. "No. I'm probably overreacting."

"Probably," she interrupts.

I scowl. "I was talking to Gina and she said something that got me thinking."

"Gina?"

I give a half smile. "I know, right? Anyway, she asked if I thought Alexander was jealous that Melanie was out with Jake. I never thought about it before, but what if Alexander likes having Melanie there whenever he needs something? Maybe he doesn't want to have to share her."

Angie listens intently. "I could see that, but I don't think that has anything to do with your relationship with Alexander."

I groan and cover my face with a pillow. "You can't leave. How am I ever going to survive without you?"

She laughs. "You'll be fine. But there is one thing you have to do for me."

I raise my eyebrows. I'm hesitant to agree to anything Angie says without knowing what it is.

"Promise me we will always spend Halloween together," she begs.

And that's all it takes for me to start the ugly cry, which makes Angie start the ugly cry. I can only imagine what people would think if they walked in to find us binging on donuts and crying.

"I'm really happy for you," I tell her after I pull myself together. "And a little jealous."

She laughs. "You could join us."

That's actually tempting, but with my career really starting to take off, I have no plans to leave Connecticut anytime soon.

Angie ends up staying for the majority of the day, and we spend most of the afternoon taking a trip down memory lane. We spend hours looking through yearbooks and photo albums. I can't believe that in a few months Angie will be thousands of miles away. Sometimes I wish I could run away to Disney World, too. Of course, I'm really happy for her and Brett. I'm expecting the proposal isn't far behind.

Several hours later, I'm finally firing up my laptop when Alexander calls.

"Hey, babe. How was your day?"

I sigh loudly. "Very unproductive. I was just going to do some research for your parents' house."

Of course, Alexander can sense my distress, so I tell him all about Angie's news and he's very understanding as always.

"I'm sorry. I know how close you two are."

Ugh. I remember when Angie went away to summer camp one year. I was lost without her and that was only for two weeks. This is going to be a whole new experience for me.

"Yeah, it's going to be hard. But I know life changes and people move on. I'm happy for her."

Alexander tells me about his day, and I start to zone out. He mentions Melanie but nothing about her and Jake. I'm curious if he asked her, but I don't want to be the one to bring it up.

"Is anything else bothering you or is it just Angie's news?"

Crap. Did I miss something he said?

"What?" I say absently.

He laughs. "I can always tell when you aren't listening."

I cringe.

"I'm sorry. I zoned out for a second."

Just then, there's a knock at my door. Crap. Mrs. Rothera is right on time as usual. I've been so distracted by Angie that I almost forgot she was supposed to stop by tonight.

"Ugh. This is exactly why I need to move," I say out loud.

"What?" he asks curiously.

"Mrs. Rothera. She wants to go over more decorating ideas."

He laughs. "I'll let you take care of that. Call me later."

I start to dig through the mess that is all over my apartment. I had all my ideas for her in a folder.

"Be right there," I call. I rush to the door and pull it open. Although, it's not Mrs. Rothera at the door, it's Jake.

Chapter Four

I'm definitely not expecting Jake to be standing outside the door when I open it. The last time he was here didn't go so well, so I'm not sure why he would come back.

"Jake. What are you doing here?"

He shoves his hands in his pockets and rocks back on his heels. "I'm sorry to stop in unexpectedly. I was in the neighborhood, and well . . . there's something I wanted to talk to you about."

Seriously? He couldn't just text or even call me?

"Okay, but I only have a few minutes. Mrs. Rothera should be here any minute."

He frowns. Mrs. Rothera doesn't care for Jake and he knows it. He walks in my apartment and starts talking right away.

"This is awkward, but I feel like I owe it to you to tell you in person."

I fold my arms tightly against my chest. I already have a feeling this has to do with Melanie.

"I've started seeing someone and . . ."

"You're seeing Melanie," I interrupt.

He opens his eyes wider. "Yes, how did you know?"

I tell him about seeing them at the café, and he looks surprised. I guess they didn't see us after all.

"Who you choose to date is your business, Jake," I say flatly.

He nods. "I know, but being that you're seeing her boss, I felt I owed it to you to be honest. And you made it clear that we would never have a chance again."

I purse my lips. I'm not sure what that has to do with him seeing Melanie. I'm trying to decide if I should warn him about her unhealthy attachment to Alexander.

"Melanie is very devoted to Alexander," I say carefully.

He nods. "I know. We've talked about him a great deal. And you."

Me?

"What could Melanie possibly say about me?"

He shrugs. "She told me how protective she is of Alexander and how she had reservations about him getting involved again so quickly after his divorce. She's not just his assistant —she's his friend."

I bite my tongue a little harder in order to stop myself from bashing Melanie. That would be completely immature and petty. Of course, it would be fun, too, but that's not the point.

"I told her that you're a good person and that you would never do anything to hurt him . . . or anyone." He trails off. There is the familiar expression of guilt on his face that I've seen before.

"Yes, I would never hurt Alexander, and from what I know about his divorce, it was a mutual decision."

He shrugs. "Yes, but she initiated it."

Okay, I'm not trying to get into a discussion about Alexander's past relationship.

"I appreciate you stopping by Jake, but I need to get some work done. It's been a very long, emotional day."

He eyes me curiously. "Everything okay?"

I exhale. "It will be. I just found out Angie and Brett are moving to Florida."

His mouth drops open. "Really? That's definitely surprising news."

I don't answer him. He knows Angie doesn't like him either because of what he did to me.

Mrs. Rothera knocks on the door before I'm able to kick Jake out. I groan as I know she will be very curious as to why he's back in my apartment again.

"Crap."

He holds up his hands. "Should I escape through a window?"

I shrug. "That's not a bad idea. Thanks for stopping by."

When I open the door, Jake says a quick hello to Mrs. Rothera before he practically races out of my apartment.

"It's not what it looks like," I say quickly before she has a chance to give me one of her famous looks of disapproval.

She smiles. "I didn't say anything."

I close the door behind her. "You didn't, but I know what you're thinking."

I pick up my laptop from my desk and bring it to the couch where she's patiently waiting. I open the folder on my desktop that I have set up for her. She's being very quiet, so quiet that it's freaking me out a little. Normally, she's rambling on about all kinds of nonsense.

"I'm sorry I don't have all of this ready for you; it's been a hectic day."

She raises an eyebrow. "Anything I can help with?"

I shake my head. "I found out Angie's moving out of state. I'm just a little sad."

She gives me a sympathetic look.

"Oh dear, that's a shame."

I hang my head. "Yeah, I don't know what I will do without her."

She pats me on the arm. "Well, you have me. I mean, in case you ever need someone to talk to."

I give her a grateful smile. "I appreciate that."

And I do appreciate it. As frustrated as I get with her always popping in, I know she means well. I turn the computer toward her so she can see the color scheme I picked out for her guest room.

"And as far as Jake goes, he just came by to tell me he's seeing someone. It doesn't bother me, but it's kind of an awkward situation."

She nods. "Of course he did. He's looking for your approval."

I snort. "I'm not sure I can give him that because he's seeing Melanie. I don't know if that's a good thing or not."

Mrs. Rothera knows all about Melanie and my complicated relationship. In fact, Melanie was the one who told her I was looking for a new place. This didn't go over well with Alexander, but somehow she managed to talk her way out of it as usual.

She's busy scrolling through my ideas on the computer. I'm wondering if she already knew about Melanie and Jake. I still don't know if she has any client-psychic confidentiality agreements.

"You should give him your blessing. That way he knows without a doubt you've moved on."

I nod. "I have moved on." I pause. "But you're right, I need to give them my blessing. And I'm glad Melanie has someone to distract her, even if it is Jake. Sometimes I feel like I have to share Alexander. It's frustrating."

I don't know why I suddenly feel the need to unload on her. I usually try to stay reserved when talking to her.

"Just be careful," she says wistfully.

"Be careful about what?" I ask.

She has a very pensive expression on her face. It's almost as if she's watching something unfold.

"Don't try too hard to push her out. There may not be romantic feelings for her, but she's important to him."

My mind wanders back to what Gina said. Maybe Alexander is jealous, and maybe he really doesn't want to share Melanie with anyone else

Mrs. Rothera finally leaves after what feels like hours, but she was actually only here for about an hour and a half. I must be really struggling with the news of Angie moving because I didn't mind her company at all tonight.

I finally crawl into bed around one o'clock after talking to Alexander for a few minutes. As I lie in my bed, I think about everything that has happened in my life since last summer. I remember this time last year Jake and I were in a very committed relationship. I truly believed we had a great future ahead of us.

Things sure have changed and I have moved on, so it would be silly to not expect Jake to do the same. Alexander is an amazing man, and I believe he loves me. Despite everything that has happened between us, I'm happy that he's bringing me home to meet his family.

I really should listen to what Angie said. We could have an awesome future ahead of us, and it's up to me to push past my insecurities and focus on that. I want to tell him how I feel about him and that I love him, too. I stretch out and pull the covers tightly around me. Spring is in the air and it's time for a fresh start and for me that means a fresh new attitude.

Chapter Five

I'm definitely a different person when the sun is out. The more I think about it, I could totally move to Florida. I'm sitting at an outdoor table at Starbucks (outdoors!), and it's glorious. As I look around, I can see that the other customers are enjoying the weather just as much as I am. Spring has come at the perfect time.

I'm busy prepping for my big night tonight, aka the night I meet Alexander's parents. I shouldn't be that worried because parents usually like me. Jake's mom and stepdad live in Boston, but I met them twice and they told Jake he should propose right away. Yeah, that certainly didn't go like they had hoped.

I asked Alexander if I had anything to worry about, and he insisted they couldn't wait to meet me.

I haven't seen Alexander in almost a week because he's been traveling for work, so I'm beyond ready for our reunion. He still hasn't mentioned anything about Melanie and Jake, and I haven't brought it up either. I'm really trying hard to have a fresh new outlook and focus on our future together. Alexander being the awesome boyfriend he is agreed to let me host a good-bye party for Angie and Brett at his house.

I spend the remainder of the morning contacting potential clients from referrals, and the best part is that I stay outside the entire time.

I change my outfit four times before finally deciding on a cute and classy high-low dress with wedges. I'm just putting on my jewelry when there's a knock at the door. Alexander is leaning against the doorframe when I open the door.

"Hi. I'm so . . ."

Before I finish talking, Alexander scoops me up in his arms and kisses me as if his life depended on it. After he places me back down on the ground, he closes his eyes and puts his forehead to mine.

"I've missed you," he whispers softly. "Next time, you have to join me because I hate being away from you for that long.

I wrap my arms around his neck. "I think that can be arranged."

His lips press hard against mine, and I know I'm going to need to touch up my makeup, but I don't care.

I run my fingers slowly down his biceps. "Do you think your mom would be devastated if we canceled on her? We could stay here."

He throws his head back. "Don't tempt me. As much as I love my parents, I would rather spend the evening alone with you."

I head to the bathroom to fix my makeup. Alexander comes up behind me and wraps his arms around my waist.

"I was serious, though, what would you say about coming with me on my next trip? I want to spend time with you without any distractions."

I smile. "I think it sounds perfect, sign me up."

We start kissing again, and I finally push him out of the bathroom so I can make myself presentable again.

What is only an hour drive feels like five hours. The knots in my stomach are getting increasingly tighter as we get closer. Alexander's talking a mile a minute about work and his recent trip. I'm trying to be the supportive girlfriend, but I'm too busy obsessing over every possible scenario that could happen tonight. I'm also making a mental list of possible excuses I can use to make a quick getaway, should I need to. I even texted Angie and asked her to be on standby in case I call with some kind of fake emergency. Of course, she thinks I'm losing it and maybe I am. I'm bringing a gorgeous bouquet of fresh flowers and a bottle of wine. I was always taught it's important to never show up empty-handed, especially the first time you're meeting your boyfriend's parents.

"You're very quiet," Alexander says, reaching for my hand. "You really don't have to be nervous. My parents are not that scary, well, maybe my mom's a little scary, but only because she's the one who always caught me getting into trouble."

I laugh nervously. "I know. I just want to make a good impression."

He kisses my hand. "You will, and I know they're going to love your ideas for the house."

"Well, I would like to get to know them before I just walk in there and start changing things. That wouldn't the best way to win them over."

A few minutes later, we pull into a long driveway on the right side of a charming two-story brick home. I have to admit it's even more stunning in person. The first thing I notice are the tall white pillars on both sides of the door and white shutters at every window. I notice that fresh bushes and flowers have been planted around the front porch, another reason I love springtime.

"Here we are," Alexander announces loudly.

I take a few deep breaths and get out of the car. There's a large wooden deck on the backside of the house. We walk up a few steps toward two French doors. Alexander holds my hand tightly in his. I take a few breaths and plaster a big smile on my face.

A taller, older version of Alexander greets us at the door. He's obviously Alexander's father, and I'm amazed at how much they look alike. Now I know what Alexander will look like in a few years, and it's definitely a good thing.

"Hello, son," he says, holding out his hand to shake.

"Hello, Father." Alexander shakes his hand, and then they hug in the typical manly kind of way. They're both smiling, so this must be some kind of inside joke I don't know about.

We all walk into the house, and immediately I start looking around to get decorating ideas. As usual, it's fun and exciting to see a brand new blank canvas.

"And who did you bring with you today?" he asks, looking past Alexander toward me.

Alexander smiles proudly.

"Dad, I would like you to meet my amazing girlfriend, Summer Peters."

Of course, I start to blush.

"It's wonderful to meet you, Mr. Williams," I say politely.

"It's very nice to meet you. I've heard quite a bit about you. And please call me Rick."

We follow Rick down a hallway and into the spacious kitchen. I immediately get excited at the possibility of giving this kitchen a fresh new start. The walls are painted a very pale yellow; it's not ugly, just outdated. The cabinets are oak, very well made, but could use a facelift.

The island is covered with a variety of appetizers, including bruschetta, vegetables, mini quiches, and a cheese platter. There's enough food to feed an army and that's just appetizers. There's a mouth-watering aroma coming from the oven.

"Where's Mom?" Alexander asks, taking a carrot from the vegetable tray. He puts the bottle of wine down on the counter.

"She ran to the market for something, should be back in a few minutes."

I'm still holding the bouquet of flowers, so I hand them to Alexander.

"Let's leave these here. I'm sure Mom will want to put them in a vase."

Rick offers us a drink, and I manage to bite my tongue to stop myself from asking him for a shot of tequila. A few minutes later, he takes us down to the basement where he proudly unveils his new man cave. Apparently, Penny

(Alexander's mother) has banished him and his sports memorabilia collection to the basement. His collection is very impressive, full of autographed football helmets, pictures, balls, etc.

"Wow. My father would love this room," I exclaim, looking around at the walls. "He's been a football coach for years."

Rick smiles mischievously. "Giants or Jets fan?"

I laugh. "Jets."

He punches the air. "Good man. Our team doesn't get the accolades they deserve. All those bandwagon fans are so disloyal. I'm a Jets fan for life."

I throw my head back in laughter. "I've heard this before."

Rick puts his arm around Alexander and pretends to whisper in his ear. "I'm liking this girl already, son."

Alexander pretends to whisper back. "Me, too."

I start to blush again. I wonder if I'm going to be blushing all day today.

While Rick and Alexander talk, I walk around and look at his collection. Obviously, I won't be redecorating anything in this basement. I hear my phone buzzing from my bag; Angie's sent me several texts asking how things are going. I excuse myself and walk back upstairs. I don't feel comfortable wandering around the house alone, so I sit down at the table in the kitchen and text her back.

So far so good. Haven't met his mom yet.

I'm just about to send another text when I hear a door shut and see an attractive brunette walking down the hall toward the kitchen carrying two grocery bags. I see she's struggling with the bags, so I rush to help her.

"Let me take one of those for you," I say, grabbing the bag before she drops it.

"Thank you."

We put the bags down and finally come face to face.

"I'm Summer," I say warmly.

For a second, I feel like she's sizing me up. I'm sure it's the typical motherly thing to do, checking out the woman who's taking her place in her son's life. But considering Alexander was married, this shouldn't be a new feeling for her. Add in the fact that her son has hired me to redecorate her home. I didn't even consider the possibility that she could have been close to Helena. What if she feels the same way about Alexander and Helena as his best friends do? They would love nothing more than for them to reconcile.

"You're the decorator."

Okay, so that was a little on the cold side, but I promised Alexander I wouldn't overreact.

And I'm your son's girlfriend but whatever. Of course, I don't say that out loud.

"Yes. I'm not sure if Alexander told you or not but I have my own company, Summer Interiors."

She starts to empty her grocery bags onto the counter.

"Yes, he did, and I've heard very good things. I'm Penny."

I can definitely see why Alexander is so good-looking. Both of his parents are attractive, and they obviously take good care of themselves.

"Where is Alexander?"

"He's downstairs with his father, enjoying the man cave."

She rolls her eyes.

"That doesn't surprise me. He comes home for the first time in months and immediately gets sucked into the basement."

"I didn't get sucked in. I'm right here," Alexander interrupts. He holds out his arms, and Penny rushes to give him a hug.

"My handsome boy," she exclaims, cupping his cheeks with her hands.

It's very sweet to watch them interact. But, I'm a little unsure of Penny and her reception of me. I know it's our first meeting, so I won't read too much into it, but I have a feeling something's off.

"This is a lot of food, Mom," Alexander says, looking at the spread on the island.

She waves her hand back and forth.

"You can never have too much food, and Anna said she may try to stop by."

Anna is Alexander's older sister; he's mentioned her a few times. Apparently, she's a busy mom of four and the PTA President.

After a few glasses of wine and about twenty mini quiches, I'm much more relaxed. When we finally sit down for dinner, I'm so full but I know how much time Penny's put into the meal, so I force myself to take a few bites.

"Mom, this is delicious," Alexander says, as he digs into the pork tenderloin and roasted potatoes.

"Thank you. I got the recipe from Melanie; her food is always a huge hit."

At the mention of Melanie, I start to choke on my potatoes. I can't believe one of my biggest fears may actually happen . . . I'm going to die from choking.

"Summer, are you okay?" Alexander shrieks.

I manage to clear my throat after chugging my entire glass of water.

"Ahem . . . yes, I'm okay. Sorry, it went down wrong."

Once I get over seeing my life flash before my eyes and the embarrassment, it hits me that Penny and Melanie are sharing recipes. It could be nothing, but it makes me start to wonder about Penny's immediate reaction to me. I thought she might have been sizing me up because I'm taking Helena's place, but that may not be the case.

"Penny, everything is delicious," I exclaim. I'm hoping she takes the bait and offers up some more information about Melanie.

"Thank you. Melanie has some fantastic recipes, both the pork and the potatoes. The key lime pie I made for dessert is also her recipe. They're all wonderful."

I glance at Alexander who's practically licking his plate. I think it's pretty clear that Penny and Melanie are friends, and that doesn't bode well for me.

Following dinner, I help Alexander clean up the dishes while his parents set up the fire pit in the backyard.

"Why are you so quiet?"

I shrug my shoulders.

"No. Tell me what's bothering you. Are you not enjoying yourself?"

I turn to face him and lean against the counter.

"I guess your mom and Melanie are friends, huh?"

He opens his mouth to say something, and then immediately closes it.

"Thank you both for helping," Penny interrupts.

Crap. I hope she didn't hear me ask about her friendship with Melanie.

"The coffee is on, and we can have dessert whenever you're ready."

Ugh, how about never. I feel like I'm going to explode. As soon as I heard the food was all from the cookbook of Melanie, I forced myself to eat almost all of it.

"Oh wow. I definitely need to make some room," I exclaim.

Alexander and I make our way outside. The subject of me redecorating hasn't come up, and I'm certainly not going to bring it up. We've talked about Anna and her family, Alexander's job, and Rick and Penny's Alaskan cruise, but nothing about me changing Penny's house. I'm getting the feeling it was all Alexander's idea and she's not really keen on the idea.

The four of us are sitting around the fire. I'm wrapped in a warm blanket, and Alexander has his arm around me.

"So, tell me again how you two met?" Penny asks.

He gives me a loving smile. "I was looking for someone to decorate the new place, and Summer Interiors came very highly recommended from the reviews. Now looking back, there was something that drew me to her. I know it was meant to be."

There I go again, blushing. Luckily, it's dark outside so they won't notice.

"I still remember our first meeting," I say, with a laugh. "When I asked him which rooms he was interested in decorating, he said all of them. I admit I was more excited about working with Alexander than about contracting a new client."

"It was the best business decision I ever made," he says, kissing my forehead.

My heart begins to flutter. It occurs to me that Melanie and Penny may be sharing recipes but Alexander loves me. I need to trust in that.

"Same for me," I say, looking into his eyes.

"That's my boy," Rick says proudly. "Good taste in teams and women." We all start to laugh, including Penny.

Alexander and I finally have a few minutes alone when Penny and Rick bring the coffee cups and plates inside.

"Can you do me a favor?" I whisper.

"Of course."

"Can you not mention the redecorating tonight? If your mom brings it up, that's one thing. I just want them to get to know me as your girlfriend first."

He smiles. "Okay, I won't say anything. At least, not tonight."

Chapter Six

*I*t's been four days since my dinner with Alexander's parents, and he's been so busy with work that I haven't seen him. Today, he's working in town and I'm meeting him at his office for lunch. I'm expecting to run into Melanie for the first time since Jake told me they were dating, and I have no idea how she's going to act toward me. Although, finding out she and Alexander's mother are buddies certainly complicates things a little more. I really shouldn't complain because the family dinner ended up being fine. Of course, the subject of me redecorating never came up, and honestly, I'm okay with that. I finally explained my feelings about it to Alexander and he was very understanding. If Penny and Rick want me to decorate their home, they can ask me themselves.

I've started planning Angie's good-bye party, and I get emotional just thinking about it. She keeps telling me we have plenty of time, but I have a feeling the big move is going to be sooner than we all expect. We've set the date for the party in three weeks, and I've already been sending invitations.

When I arrive at the office, Melanie is sitting at her desk staring at her laptop. I can hear Alexander talking on his phone in his office.

"Hello, Melanie."

She turns around and gives me a half wave, half smile.

"Alexander's on an important call. You may have to wait for a little while, or you can come back if you have something else to do."

I nod and sit down in one of the chairs. It's not surprising that she wants to get rid of me as quickly as possible.

"I'll just wait for now."

She continues working while I silently look at my phone.

"What did you think of Penny and Rick?"

I'm not sure I feel comfortable talking about Alexander's parents with Melanie. What if I say something the wrong way and it gets twisted? She will totally use that against me. Whether she's in a new relationship or not, I know she's still threatened by me.

"They were great."

She gives me a smug smile.

"They are. I got to know them really well when we went to Key West together."

Huh? Key West? She went on a trip with them?

Once again, I'm not going to make a big deal out of this. And even if I am upset, I'm going to pretend I'm *not* upset.

"Oh, by the way, your pork tenderloin recipe was delicious," I say sweetly. I have every intention to kill her with kindness.

She laughs. "Did Penny serve the pork again? She makes it every time they entertain. Did she make the mini quiches this time?

Holy crap. I figured those quiches were from the frozen food section at Costco. I'm not going to tell her I ate twenty of them or that I loved them.

"Yes, they were good."

Once again, we're both quiet. I wonder if there will ever come a time when things aren't awkward between us.

"So, how are things going with Jake?"

She raises an eyebrow.

"Things are good."

I'm totally going to take this opportunity and run with it.

"That's what Jake said when he stopped by. I'm really happy for him . . . for both of you. I hope Jake finds as much happiness as I have with Alexander."

I force myself to keep from laughing at her expression. I think she may be in shock to hear that I'm publicly giving them my blessing. I still believe she was hoping I would get jealous and try to get back together with him. That would have freed Alexander so she could have him all to herself.

"I am happy with him. So much that sometimes it's hard to concentrate on work. I would love to spend more time with him."

"What makes it so hard to concentrate?" Alexander asks.

He has a worried expression on his face.

"Her new boyfriend," I tease. She glares at me. If looks could kill, I'd probably be dead.

He shakes his head.

"None of that right now. We have to get this acquisition completed. I need you all in right now."

Hearing Alexander talk about not losing Melanie doesn't surprise me, and for some reason, Mrs. Rothera's advice keeps repeating in my head. I can't force Melanie out, and as much as I don't want to, I have to share him. At least for right now.

"You ready?" he asks, dragging me out of my thought.

I nod. "Yep."

"We'll be back in an hour," he tells Melanie. "If you need me, call."

Crap. I'm expecting her to call before we even get in the car.

I can tell Alexander is distracted today, and I know it's because of all he has going on with work. We're almost halfway to the restaurant when he brings up my conversation with Melanie.

"What were you two discussing? It seemed like everyone was on their best behavior and not one punch was thrown."

I give him a half smile. "Actually, we were talking about her and Jake."

This is the first time the subject of Melanie and Jake has come up since they've officially become a couple. It's obvious how uncomfortable Alexander is.

"Yeah, I'm sorry about that. I'm sure it's not easy for you."

The thing is it doesn't bother me as much I thought it would. I think this is a good sign that I'm moving past everything that happened with Jake last summer. If anything, it seems to bother Alexander more than it bothers me.

"Believe it or not, it doesn't really bother me. We're both moving on; that's what's supposed to happen."

Granted, I never expected him to move on with my boyfriend's assistant, but when it comes to things Jake does, I'm not surprised anymore.

"Not to change the subject, but I didn't realize Melanie and your mom were so close, other than sharing recipes."

He shrugs nonchalantly. "Melanie's been working with me for a while. She's met my family on several occasions. I wouldn't say they're friends, though, maybe a message every few months."

"Well, she made it sound like they were very close. She mentioned going on the family trip to Key West."

Alexander looks uncomfortable. "It's not what you think."

"How do you know what I'm thinking?" I ask curiously.

I can see how agitated he's becoming, and maybe I should just drop it. It really isn't important anymore.

"My sister was getting married in Key West, and we were closing a huge deal at work. Melanie came with me, and we spent most of the time working. It wasn't anything more than that."

I look out the window without saying anything.

"Melanie seems to think it was more or she wouldn't have tried to rub it in my face. Well, that and being besties with your mom."

Alexander exhales loudly. "I'm sorry, Summer. I don't know what else to do here. Neither of you like the other, and I'm stuck in the middle."

I feel guilty for a half a second, but I refuse to explain myself again. I can't count how many times I've tried with Melanie. It started with smug comments, selling me out to Mrs. Rothera, and now she's dating my ex-boyfriend. I'm not the one instigating this.

"I never intended to put you in the middle. I do realize she's going to be a major part of our lives. That is unless she lets Jake take over her life."

He frowns. "I appreciate that you understand, and I know how difficult it is. Melanie knows me, she knows my business, and it would be a nightmare trying to train someone else. I need her."

I would be lying if I say that didn't sting a bit.

We finally pull up at the restaurant. Talk about perfect timing. It's now clear that *if* Alexander and I are in this for the long haul I will always be sharing him. I would never make him choose, and honestly, if I did, I'm not sure he would choose me.

Chapter Seven

$\mathcal{I}$ stare at my computer screen. I could be dreaming right now, although it feels more like a nightmare. I'm in a state of shock when I see an email from Helena asking for a meeting to discuss the contract. I really believed we were past this and it wasn't happening. I guess I was wrong.

I could tell her my schedule is full and I'm not taking any more clients. That would be the nicer and much more professional way of saying "you snooze, you lose." The problem with this is that my schedule is not that full right now. Other than decorating Mrs. Rothera's bedrooms, I have one other project getting ready to start. And that's all until the summer. I have the time for Helena's apartment, and I can always use the business.

I groan as I send her a response agreeing to the meeting.

I'm sure it's going to be fine. The last thing I heard was that she reconciled with her hot French boyfriend and she's happy in her relationship. And the good thing about decorating her place is I can get rid of all the pictures of her and Alexander. I wouldn't throw them away, but I would pack them safely in a box never to be seen again. Helena was very specific about wanting a fresh new look in her home, and that's what she's going to get. Now if only I can stay sane throughout the whole project, then I will consider it a success.

As much as I'm not looking forward to dealing with Helena and her high-maintenance ways, I've decided it's better than putting up with Melanie. Ugh. I can't believe I'm thinking this way. Helena is truly the lesser of two evils. I pick up the phone to call Alexander.

At first, I don't think Alexander was happy with the idea of me working with her, but he doesn't seem to care now. It could be that he's so preoccupied with work that he doesn't hear me when I tell him about Helena contacting me. I can hear him typing on his laptop and another phone ringing in the background. We get off the phone after talking for maybe three minutes, or rather, I talked for three minutes.

"I called it months ago," Gina says smugly. "That girl has had her sights on your man for a while now. She succeeded in getting rid of the wife, and you're next."

Gina, Angie, and I are at dinner, and I just told them about the family dinner and Melanie's claims of being best friends with Penny.

"Gina, why do you have to be so harsh?" Angie yells.

She rolls her eyes. "It's not harsh, it's the facts. I told you that girl was trouble. You know I can make it all go away, don't you?"

Angie and I glance at each other, and she shakes her head. Let's just say Gina's uncle has his own ways of getting people to behave. One call from Gina and my problems with Melanie would probably disappear, which isn't a bad idea. But if that ever got back to Alexander, it would be the end of that.

"Alexander would probably never forgive me for that."

Gina pulls the crust off her piece of Italian bread and dips it in the olive oil.

"So, does this tramp like Alexander or Jake?"

I giggle. "She's not a tramp . . . at least, I don't think she is. I really don't know anything about her personal life, other than she seems to covet the men I'm involved with." I pause. "And to answer your question, I don't know who she likes. If I had to guess, I think she's in love with Alexander and is only using Jake to piss me off and make Alexander jealous."

Gina pounds on the table. "And you're just going to let her get away with this?"

I glance at Angie who's been surprisingly quiet. She looks perplexed.

"What's up with you?" I ask her, clearly ignoring Gina's outburst.

She's playing with the straw in her glass.

"We set our moving date. We're leaving in three weeks."

We're all silent, even Gina who has clearly forgotten about the revenge plot she was planning in her mind.

"I knew it would be sooner than expected," I say sadly. "That's why I set the party so soon. Once you and Brett set your minds on something, it's usually done quickly.

She has a pained look on her face.

"Yeah, we're kind of annoying, aren't we?"

"Hell yeah, you are," Gina chimes in. "It gives us procrastinators a bad rep."

We all laugh. I'm glad Gina's here for the comic relief on what would be a sad afternoon. I hate to say it, but I'd almost rather talk about Gina's possible revenge plan than the fact that my best friend will be thousands of miles away in a few weeks.

"Please, can we talk about something else?" Angie begs.

I may as well take this opportunity to give them the low down on my latest career dilemma.

"Helena requested a meeting to go over the contract I sent her. I guess she wants me to decorate her apartment after all."

"She did?" Angie squawks. "I would've bet she was playing you the whole time."

"Seriously, you mean to tell me there isn't one decorator in all of Manhattan?" Gina adds.

I shrug my shoulders. "I guess since both Alexander and Nick hired me, she wants to follow suit."

While Gina and Angie discuss the possible reasons why Helena is hiring me, I zone out.

So far, this spring isn't turning out the way I had hoped. Melanie is still intertwined in my relationship and now involved with my ex, Helena wants me to be her decorator, and my best friend is leaving in three weeks. Huh, maybe I will just have to look forward to summer.

I arrive at Nick's restaurant earlier than I expected. You never know with New York City traffic. Helena and I agreed to meet here because it's a great central location and the food is amazing, not to mention we know the owners. It also doesn't hurt for her to see some of my work as a reminder that I'm good at what I do.

"Well hello, stranger," Nick says, greeting me at the door. "Where are you hiding my best friend?"

Hmm . . . that's funny. However, it does make me feel better knowing that I'm not the only one who isn't seeing much of Alexander.

"I have no idea, but when you find him, let me know."

He starts to laugh.

"He's closing a huge deal right now, so I'm sure he'll resurface as soon as that's complete."

He nods. "I spoke with him about a week ago, and he sounded really overwhelmed. It will pay off in the end, right?"

"I hope so. He really needs to slow down, but at least he has Melanie to help him."

Okay, so I know that was a sly way of bringing up the fact that Melanie is with my boyfriend more than I am.

Nick gives me a curious look. "Is someone feeling a little insecure in their relationship?"

I laugh. "It wouldn't be the first time. Sometimes it's hard having to share Alexander with Melanie."

He purses his lips. "That's what Helena used to say to Caroline all the time."

Damn, he actually took the bait. I hope this doesn't come back to bite me.

"What do you mean?"

He shakes his head. "First of all, I know what you're thinking. Trust me when I tell you there's nothing romantic between Xander and Melanie. However, he does depend on her . . . probably more than he should and she latches onto that. If anything, I think it gives her some false hope that they could be more someday."

"So, you think he leads her on?"

He shakes his head. "No, he just makes it very obvious how much he depends on her."

I'm just about to ask his advice on how to handle the situation when he's summoned from the kitchen.

When I sit down at our table, I take out my laptop and open the file for Helena. I stare at the screen, but I'm really thinking about what Nick said. Everyone, including Alexander himself, insists there's nothing romantic there, so it just comes down to me being secure enough in how he feels about me.

"Hello, Summer."

I look up to see Helena, the Swedish goddess, standing next to me. She's wearing a gray and white off-the-shoulder sweater, and her hair is up in a half bun on top of her head. She's as stunning as ever.

"Hi," I say cheerfully.

"Thanks for the meeting. I would have contacted you sooner, but my schedule wouldn't allow it. And Jacques and I went on a short holiday."

I smile. I can see how happy she is.

"I'm glad everything worked out for you two."

She nods. "So am I. Shall we look over everything? I have another appointment following this."

Shockingly, Helena and I have a very productive meeting. She seems to be receptive to most of my ideas, or it could be that she's just telling me what I want to hear. And before we end our meeting, she signs the contract. So, I guess this means she's officially my new client. Wow, who would have thought I'd be working with my boyfriend's ex-wife? Oh well, I'm not going to let it concern me. She's moved on and so has Alexander. I'm just going to keep my fingers crossed that everything will go smoothly.

Chapter Eight

$\mathcal{T}$he last few days have been exhausting. Ever since Angie announced that they were moving in a few weeks, I've been in full party planning mode. The planning has helped to distract me from the sadness of her leaving. I even rented a karaoke machine as a throwback to our college days. We loved going to karaoke night, so I thought it would be a fun way to celebrate. I feel like I could sleep for days, so when I arrive home from the city, I'm ready to crash. Until I see the note Mrs. Rothera left for me on my door.

Please stop by my place when you get home.

-Mrs. R

I groan loudly. On the other hand, if I look on the bright side, at least she didn't come to my apartment unannounced. I'm sure this has something to do with her apartment; maybe she's changed her mind on the style already. Based on the last project I did with her, she changed her mind at least four different times, so it's probably that time.

I shouldn't complain because our last interaction went really well. I actually enjoyed her company.

And if she asks me how my apartment search is going, she'll be happy to know that I haven't had time to look for a new place in days, so as of right now, I'm not going anywhere.

I slowly make my way back downstairs, and when I approach the door, I hear music playing. This isn't the first time I've heard this music. It's a weird mixture of sounds, like different instruments, chanting, and humming. She claims this is meditation music but to me it sounds like a bunch of noise. I knock loudly on the door, and sure enough, she answers a few seconds later. I have no idea how she hears me when that music is playing, but she does every time.

"Sorry to bother you. I just got your note."

She has a very calm and serene look on her face. I guess the meditation noise-music works.

"Thank you for coming," she says calmly, actually it sounds more like she's singing. I walk into her dark living room, and she quickly turns on the lights.

"I wanted to talk to you about my bedroom. I'm just not feeling what we discussed."

I knew it. I take my tablet out of my bag to get ready to jot down her new ideas. At least I didn't put a lot of time into this yet.

"I hope you don't think I'm being difficult."

I stare at my tablet trying not to make any kind of eye contact with her. I'm not going to answer that. It's probably better than trying to lie my way out of it.

"What did you have in mind instead of the Moroccan?" I ask, changing the subject before she asks me again.

She sits down and begins taking slow, deep breaths. What the hell is she doing? It looks like she's going into labor.

"I'm thinking the islands of the South Pacific. Maybe some palms, floral, bamboo. Oh, maybe I should get an aquarium? That would definitely give it an island feel."

An aquarium? She can't be serious. I quickly type up the notes as she's talking.

"Okay, I will get started on this."

I head for the door when she stops me.

"Forgive me for asking, but you seem very concerned about something."

I laugh loudly. "When am I not concerned? It seems like I'm always worrying about something."

Mrs. Rothera doesn't seem to find this as funny as I do.

"Angie's leaving in a few weeks, and I guess I've been going through a rough time thinking about her being so far away."

She nods her head, but I know she can see right through me. All of a sudden, something comes over me and I feel the need to completely unload on her. It feels as if the words begin to pour out of my mouth like vomit.

"And there's the whole thing with Alexander and Melanie . . . again." As soon as I say it out loud, I immediately hope I don't regret it.

"Ah yes, but the last I heard there wasn't an Alexander and Melanie. I thought she was dating Jake."

I roll my eyes.

"She *is* dating Jake. For what reasons, I don't know other than in an attempt to make me jealous. Anyway, regardless of whom she's dating, she's Alexander's assistant and that's a big deal to him."

"You're afraid you're going to lose him, aren't you? You're afraid he's going to move on like Jake did."

I rub my forehead. "I guess so. The thing is Alexander has already told me he loves me. And I'm the one who hasn't said it back to him yet."

She tries to hide her smile. I know she's enjoying the fact I'm finally confiding in her.

"Do you love Alexander?"

I take a deep breath and lean my head back. I know how I feel about him, but for some reason I'm holding back on admitting my feelings out loud and to myself.

"It's difficult to open up your heart after it's been broken," she adds. "You're entitled to feel this way."

"It's very difficult. And yes, I do love Alexander, and that terrifies me."

After I say it, I feel like a weight has been lifted off my shoulders. I'm actually wondering if Mrs. Rothera put something in the air. She's always using different kinds of essential oils, and maybe tonight she's put some kind of calming blend into the air. Holy crap, maybe she's drugging me. Maybe it's a truth serum or love potion? Either way, I actually finally admitted it. I'm in love with Alexander. But now what? Am I going to be okay with Melanie always being here? I thought I was okay with it. I guess I had just accepted it because we were just casually dating, but now this is serious. This is my future . . . our future, and I really need to think hard about this before I let myself get in any deeper.

"You need to tell him how you feel," Mrs. Rothera demands. I almost forgot I was still in her apartment. Seriously, what did she put in the air?

"You mean that I'm in love with him."

She nods slowly. "Yes—but also how you're feeling about the situation with Melanie."

I frown. "I've done this already. He knows how I feel."

"He knows you're not sure you want to move forward in this relationship?"

I furrow my brow. "I never said that."

"You didn't have to say it. You're having a lot of doubts and have been for a while. There's another woman in his life— maybe not in the same manner as you, but she's there and it doesn't appear she will be going anywhere. Unless, you speak up."

This really sucks. How am I supposed to tell him I love him, and then tell him he needs to choose between us? Is that really fair to him? But is it fair to me?

"You told me I shouldn't push her out," I remind her.

"I did tell you that. But if it's weighing on you this much, you can't stay silent. You're visibly distraught about it, and I believe you can do it in a way that's not *forcing* him to choose. Just be honest and let it come from the heart."

I finally crawl into bed after what seems like one of the longest days of my life. Mrs. Rothera was really helpful tonight, and now I feel super guilty for being so negative toward her. Yes, she's nosy and sometimes the unsolicited advice is too much. But, she also cares about people, and for some reason she especially cares about me. Tonight, she acted like a supportive friend and not a nosy neighbor-psychic. And she swore up and down she didn't release any kind of soothing chemical into the air.

Now comes the million-dollar question: When do I talk to Alexander about my concerns? Right now, he's so busy with this acquisition I think it will just add to his stress levels. I certainly don't want to be the cause of that.

In the meantime, I can put all my attention into my projects for both Mrs. Rothera and Helena, and of course, Angie's good-bye party. I also can't forget about finding a new place to live—I still want a fresh new start, but I need to find the right place to start over. I'm not going to rush into anything, because I'm learning that rushing into things is not the best idea.

Chapter Nine

$\mathcal{S}$ometimes all you need is a good shopping trip to clear your mind. And for me, this is exactly what I need. Gina was supposed to meet me to shop for a going away present for Angie, but something urgent suddenly came up and with Gina that could be anything. As I walk through the mall, I'm kind of glad she canceled. It gives me a chance to really think. It's not like I haven't thought about how to handle the Alexander-Melanie situation, it's practically been monopolizing every waking moment I have. The good news is when I spoke to him this morning he told me they would finally be wrapping up this deal today and tomorrow, and we're having dinner tomorrow night to celebrate. I'm not sure if that's the right time to have our little talk or if I should wait, but I've never been very good about keep things bottled up inside. And usually I'm so transparent I end up blabbing my feelings anyway.

The other night with Mrs. Rothera is the perfect example of this.

I would normally talk to Angie about this, but she's so busy with the move and I don't want to give her anything more to worry about. As it is, she's been sending me multiple texts checking up on me every day. I feel like the little child whose best friend is moving away. I have this image of myself hugging a stuffed animal and chasing after the moving van as it drives down the street. Seriously, I'm an adult and I need to act like one. It's okay (and natural) to be sad, but I can't let it consume my whole life. Things change and people move on. This is just part of life.

I'm in Pottery Barn looking for something for Angie's new place when I see Melanie.

Crap! This is the last thing I want right now. I try to hide behind a tall display of throw pillows but I'm too late.

"Summer?"

I crawl out from behind the pillows and try to act surprised to see her. I know she caught me trying to hide from her.

"Oh, hi, Melanie," I say, trying to sound surprised to see her.

Ugh, I'm really not a good liar.

"Looking for something back there?" she asks smugly. I wonder if I'd get arrested if I accidentally punched her. I know that's not the mature way to handle this, but it was just a random thought.

I ignore her snarky comment and change the subject away from me trying to hide from her.

"Hey, congrats on the acquisition. Alexander told me it's being finalized today."

Her smugness seems to disappear for a moment. "Yes, we did it. Alexander was so sweet and gave me the rest of the day off today."

"You guys worked really hard. I'm sure it's well deserved."

She nods. "So, what are you doing? Are you here to get Penny a birthday present, too?"

Penny—it doesn't take a genius to know she's talking about Alexander's mom. Of course, I didn't know it was her birthday.

"No, actually a good-bye present for Angie. She's moving soon, and I wanted to get her something for her new home."

"I guess great minds think alike. Penny loves this store."

I force a smile. Maybe I'm making a huge deal out of nothing. So what if she and Penny are friends. She's allowed to be friends with whomever she wants. That doesn't change how Alexander feels about me.

"Who doesn't love Pottery Barn?" I say loudly.

Of course, I immediately think of the episode of *Friends* where Phoebe hates Pottery Barn. I start to giggle, and Melanie gives me a funny look.

"Sorry, I just remembered something funny."

Obviously, she doesn't remember the episode.

"Well, I better get back to shopping," I say awkwardly.

I start to walk away, and she follows me. Really? What else does this girl want from me? "Did you need something else?" I ask, looking back at her.

She glares at me. "You really don't like me, do you?"

She really wants to do this now—in the middle of Pottery Barn.

"I never said that," I say calmly.

She snorts. "Come on, it's no secret how we feel about each other. Sure, we try to play nice for Alexander's sake, but it is what it is."

Okay, so I don't disagree with her, but I'm still not sure what she's trying to accomplish by doing this now.

"The fact is you're Alexander's assistant and I'm his girlfriend. We have no choice but to coexist."

"And you hate that."

I grit my teeth. "What do you want, Melanie? What's the point of your infatuation with Alexander anyway? I thought you were dating Jake, remember Jake, my ex-boyfriend?"

She gives me a wicked smile. "You mean the one who broke up with you."

That was a low blow. In this situation, I could do one of two things: I could start screaming at her in the middle of Pottery Barn and maybe something childish like pulling her hair, or I could calmly and rationally walk away and include it in my conversation with Alexander. I have to do what I have to do.

"Yes, Jake and I broke up. Of course, I was disappointed at first, but then I met Alexander and . . . well, you know the rest."

It's my turn to give her a smug smile and remind her that Alexander and I are in relationship despite her many previous attempts to break up our relationship.

I decide to leave the store and get away from Melanie before I do or say something I can't take back. Now I wish Gina had met me after all. She would have had no mercy on Melanie, and of course, I could easily remind Alexander that I can't control what Gina does. I've finally decided that enough is enough, we all tried to make it work, but it's obviously not going to. What the next step is, I don't know.

"Are you serious? Oh man, I wish I was there," Gina yells.

After my escape from Pottery Barn, I went to the office I share with Gina and told her about my run-in with Melanie.

"She probably wouldn't have acted like that if you were there. She's really good at making it look like she's completely innocent."

"I can't believe she brought up the fact that Jake broke up with you. Just proves what a bitch she really is."

I don't disagree.

"There's something that's bothering me, though," I say. "She just doesn't seem to be that into Jake. It's almost like . . ."

"Like what?" she asks.

"I don't know—I'm just starting to wonder if they're really dating."

"You think it's a setup?"

I shrug my shoulders.

"It might be. Maybe they plotted this whole thing to make Alexander and me jealous? I wouldn't put it past Melanie, but I would be surprised if Jake did something like this."

She has a disgusted look on her face. "I wouldn't be surprised at all. He's been trying to win you back for a while."

Gina answers a call, and I rock back and forth in my chair. Could they really be faking this? Jake was so convincing when he showed up at my apartment to tell me, but what if that was his way of trying to make me jealous? And Melanie would stop at nothing to get Alexander's attention, including make him worry he could possibly lose her to an exciting new relationship.

If this theory doesn't pan out, it's still very obvious that Melanie is not that into Jake. And if that's true and she's just playing Jake . . . well, let's just say I'm a firm believer in karma.

"So, what's the plan?" Gina asks.

I bite my lip. I don't know, but somehow I need to find out the truth. This could be the only way to prove what Melanie is really capable of.

"And what if you're wrong?"

"If I'm wrong and things go south for Alexander and me, well then, I guess we were never meant to be anyway."

Chapter Ten

*A*lexander always goes out of his way to make everything perfect. When I arrive at his house, I'm greeted with candles and Chinese lanterns hanging outside on the deck. He has a table set up outside, and he ordered dinner from my favorite Greek restaurant. I look around and I'm completely speechless. Another reason I love spring so much is being able to enjoy evenings like this.

I find Alexander in his office.

"Everything looks amazing," I say, leaning against the doorframe.

He looks up from his laptop. I walk behind his desk and lean down to give him a kiss. He quickly pulls me into his lap and kisses me with more force than usual.

"I've missed you," he whispers.

I cup his chin with my hand and kiss him again. "I've missed you more."

I sit in his lap for a while, and he tells me all about the big win for his company. I knew it was important, but I had no idea just how important. The way Alexander makes it sound, this deal has set them up for five years. I can see the relief on his face and he's back to his normal self. He's in such good mood I don't know if I have the heart to bring up my issues with Melanie.

"You hungry?" he asks.

I nod, and we make our way outside to the romantic dinner he has planned for us.

I'm just digging into my Greek salad when he asks me what's been happening with me. I laugh nervously because I don't know where to start between signing the contract with Helena, Angie moving soon, my love for him, and last but not least the almost-brawl with Melanie in Pottery Barn.

"I suppose I should give you the bad news first." I pause. "Well, it's not completely bad news, but it may come with some uncomfortable feelings and emotions."

He gives me a curious look.

"Okay, give me the news."

I take a sip of my wine. "Helena and I met at Nick's for lunch and to discuss the contract."

He raises his eyebrows. "Did she sign it?"

I nod quickly.

"She did, finally."

"So you're going to decorate my ex-wife's home?" he asks with a fake laugh. "Never in a million years did I see that one coming."

I cringe. "Neither did I, but this is all your fault. You went and referred me out to all your friends and you have the same friends as Helena. Don't get me wrong, I appreciate all the referrals, but truthfully, I didn't think she was going to go through with it and hire me. And she seems kind of . . . easy to work with."

He sips his wine. "I guess love does that to people. It makes you strive to be a better person. I'm glad she's found that someone new, and I wish her all the happiness in the world. Just like I've found with you."

I take a deep breath. It's now or never. This perfect weather and this amazing setup makes me want to tell him how I feel. I'm so nervous my palms are sweating and my mouth is dry. I shouldn't be this nervous, he's already told me how he feels, so I know he will be happy. I don't have to worry about rejection.

"I'm so sorry I've been unavailable lately. I promise it won't be like that all the time, some deals require more time and attention."

"You don't have to explain anything," I insist. "I know how important your work is."

He takes my hand in his. "Not as important as you. I know I've already told you this, but I love you, Summer."

I close my eyes and take a deep breath. "I love you, too."

The next few minutes are so surreal. I'm about to explain my feelings more in depth when he jumps out of his chair and pulls me into his arms.

"Whoa. If I had known you would have had this kind of reaction, I would have said it sooner."

He laughs. "You needed time and I respect that. I wasn't going to push you even though I couldn't wait for you to say it. Do you know how happy I am right now?"

I can see how happy he is, and I feel the same way. Truthfully, I haven't felt this happy in a long time. Even though in the back of my mind I know we still need to talk about Melanie. Sure, things are good now and we're having a wonderful night together, but what happens the next time a big project comes up or the next time Melanie tries to get under my skin. We need to have this conversation, but not tonight. I don't want to be the one to mess this up.

After dinner, Alexander puts *Grease 2* (our favorite movie) on and we curl up on the couch together. I've decided that I need to do everything I can to make this work. A man like Alexander doesn't come along every day. If anything, I should probably admire and respect his loyalty. He's definitely been loyal to Melanie, and she has to him.

Normally, I would be breaking out into song and dance to "Cool Rider" but my mind is still wandering.

"Hey, are you all right?"

I stare at him for a second.

"What? Oh yeah, just daydreaming."

He looks concerned and sits up.

"You had a very worried look on your face."

Hmm . . . I guess I didn't try hard enough to hide my distraction.

He pauses the movie and turns to face me. Crap! He's going to do this now. Why couldn't I just enjoy our evening instead of overthinking everything?

"You know I can tell by your expression. Something has you worried."

I cringe. He won't believe me if I say nothing's wrong. Now is my chance, and I need to do this in the kindest way I possibly can.

"I didn't want to talk about this tonight. Everything has been so perfect." I look down at my hands in order to avoid his curious stare.

"You know you can tell me anything."

I nod slowly. Here goes nothing.

"Did Melanie tell you we ran into each other in Pottery Barn?"

"Noooo. Did something happen between you two?"

I tell him all about our run-in except I leave out the part about me hiding behind the pillows. He listens intently as I explain my feelings.

"I'm not trying to give you an ultimatum, but I don't see how this is going to work. We've all tried, and things aren't any better between us."

Alexander is silent. He doesn't look mad, but he is visibly upset.

"Summer, are you asking me to let Melanie go?"

I grit my teeth. How do I answer this? Yes, this would be ideal unless there was some way she would lay off but it never stops.

"I'm not going to force you to do anything," I say bluntly. "But if you have another suggestion, I'm all ears. I've told you how I feel about you, and I want more than anything for this to work out between us. I just don't want to feel like I come second in your life."

"You don't," he insists. "I told you I was sorry I've been so busy."

"It's not about your work," I interrupt. "It's Melanie. And how she can't separate being your assistant and butting in to your personal life. She went out of her way to tell me she was at the store to buy your mom a birthday present."

"That's my fault. I've been so busy that I haven't had a chance to shop for her. The gift is from me, not from Melanie."

I shake my head. "See what I mean. She could have told me that, but she conveniently left that part out because she was trying so hard to make me believe she's buddies with Penny."

I know this is all making sense to him. I can almost see the wheels turning in his brain.

"Okay, I will talk to her."

I snort. "Again? Sure, things will get better for a while, and then it will happen all over again. She's got it out for me. Don't forget she told Mrs. Rothera about me moving out. Oh, and I don't believe she and Jake are really dating. I think it's all a ploy they set up to make us jealous." I don't know where this comes from, but I'm on a roll. I've come this far, I might as well put it all out there.

He puts his face in his hands. "Do you really believe they would pretend to be in a relationship?"

I fold my arms defensively. "I wouldn't put anything past either of them at this point."

It's obvious that the mood has changed once again at the mention of Melanie. This is exactly the point I'm trying to make. How long is this going to go on? Are we going to spend the remainder of our relationship arguing over this? As bummed as I am that this conversation has ruined our night, it had to be done.

"Please say something," I beg.

He's still looking at the carpet.

"I understand where you're coming from, and I never wanted you to feel like you come second. I don't know how many times I have to apologize for her behavior, but you're right. Something has to change."

My heart starts beating a mile a minute, and my mouth is dry. Would he really choose her? Maybe deep down he really does have feelings for her and doesn't realize it?

He puts his hand on my cheek. "I promise you everything's going to be okay."

I really wish I could believe him. In the meantime, I need to get to the bottom of this lingering question, and there's only one person who can answer it for me. Jake.

Chapter Eleven

*J*ake seemed really happy to get my phone call, and when I asked him to meet me, he seemed very eager. I didn't tell Alexander I was going to contact him, but I need to find out what Melanie is up to.

After our amazing evening together ended up being not so amazing, Alexander promised me he would fix everything. I don't know what he meant by that, but I'm hoping we can finally get some kind of resolution. I barely got any sleep last night thinking about all of this and about what I need to say to Jake.

I'm sitting outside (of course, any excuse to enjoy the good weather) at the same café where Angie and I saw Jake and Melanie together. I arrived a little early so I could follow up on some emails and finalize a few things for Angie's party. When I look up, I see Jake walking toward the table.

Show time.

"Hi, Jake. Thanks for meeting me."

He gives me a warm smile. "Of course. I was glad to hear from you."

He sits down and orders a drink. After a bit of small talk, he cuts to the chase.

"So, what did you want to talk about?" He's practically on the edge of his chair. I wonder what he's expecting me to say.

"Well, first of all, I hope Melanie doesn't get upset about you being here."

He gets a funny look on his face. "Why would she be upset?"

I cringe. "Let's just say Melanie and I probably won't be allowed back into Pottery Barn."

"What do you mean?"

I give him a curious look. "She didn't tell you about this?"

He shakes his head. "Um . . . no."

Of course she didn't tell him. I wouldn't be surprised if they haven't spoken in days.

"What happened?"

I tell him about our altercation. He looks angry when I tell him about what she said about him breaking up with me.

"I don't understand why she would say that."

I snort. "Oh, I can answer that, because she loves to get under my skin any chance she can get."

He looks away and doesn't say anything. Here's my chance to finally get to the bottom of all of this.

"Is everything all right with you two?"

He looks back at me. "Yeah. Why do you ask?"

I shrug my shoulders. "I don't know. Despite everything that happened with us, I want you to be happy. Just because Melanie and I don't get along doesn't mean I don't wish you well."

He folds his hands on the table. "I still wish I could take it all back. I know I've told you this before but I would give anything to change last summer. I made the biggest mistake of my life when I ended things with you."

I reach across the table and put my hands on his.

"I know. Unfortunately, we can't change the past even if we wanted to."

He takes my hands in his. "There's always a chance. And don't you want someone who will be devoted to you and only you."

I knew it. Wait until I tell Angie and Gina.

"I'm confused. First of all, Alexander is devoted to me and you're with Melanie now."

He shakes his head. "I'm not seeing Melanie. We went out a few times, but it just wasn't meant to be. She's in love with Alexander and I'm . . . well, I'm still in love with you."

It's my turn to be speechless. I'm not surprised to hear him say he's in love with me, but I am a little surprised to hear him say that Melanie is in love with Alexander. She obviously shared this bit of information with him.

"So, you two have been lying this whole time?"

"The whole thing was a stupid idea," he interrupts. "We started talking at the restaurant opening, and it was really cool. After we got to talking, we admitted that we had feelings for other people. Melanie came up with the idea to try to make you guys jealous, and I went along with it."

I shake my head. "Jake, you even came to my apartment to tell me you were seeing her."

"I know. Anyway, it obviously didn't go as planned and I just decided to back off. She's been trying to keep it going because Alexander didn't like the idea at all. She thinks he's finally showing his true feelings."

I laugh loudly. "He's been worried about how it was affecting me."

"Summer, don't you see it?" he asks. "Doesn't it bother you that she's always there?"

There's no way I'm admitting anything to him. By him going along with this plan, he's just proven to me that he can't be trusted. He will probably run back to Melanie with everything I tell him.

"She's his assistant, that's it. He loves me, and I'm in love with him."

Jake nods his head. "I'm sorry I lied to you and for everything." He pauses. "I truly hope it works out the way you want it to. I wish you nothing but happiness."

"Thanks."

A few minutes later, I make up an excuse to leave, because truthfully, the sight of him disgusts me. Now that I have this information I'm prepared for whatever happens next. I can only hope that Alexander loves me enough to make the right decision.

"We told you they were playing you," Angie says loudly. I pretend to cover my ears, and she throws piece of crumpled paper at me. Ugh. I'm really going to miss teasing her about how loud she is.

Gina is leaning back in her chair, smacking her gum as usual. "Both of them are scum. Now can I make a call?"

"No," Angie and I yell at the same time. We all start laughing.

"I appreciate the gesture, but I don't think threats of cement shoes are the answer."

She grins.

"So, what are you going to do?" Angie asks.

I exhale. "I'm going to wait on Alexander. He says he's going to take care of it, and I have to trust him."

"He will. That man loves you," Angie insists.

I smile. "I know. I just hope that's enough." I stop. "Anyway, let's talk about something else, like this good-bye bash we're having. I have a few fun surprises planned."

Tears well up in Angie's eyes. "I just can't believe we're talking about this."

I clear my throat and try my best to keep myself from crying.

"You're the one who's ditching us for sunshine and theme parks, so you only have yourself to blame," Gina says sarcastically.

Leave it to Gina to take an emotional moment and turn it into a joke, but it worked. Angie starts laughing before her tears begin to fall. Unfortunately, I know this is just the beginning of the tears.

Chapter Twelve

J'm rushing around trying to finish the last-minute details for this party. I'm really not that great at party planning. That's always been Angie's thing. Tonight is the good-bye party for Angie and Brett, and there are going to be even more surprises than I was planning. Brett called me a few nights ago and told me he was planning to propose to Angie. We have it all set up for him to pop the question tonight at the party. Angie doesn't really like surprises, but I have no doubt she won't mind this one. I really appreciate him trusting me enough to tell me. Of course, I promised him I would keep it a surprise and so far so good.

Alexander has been working in his office for most of the day while I've been dealing with caterers and decorations. At least the karaoke is ready to go. I'm so tempted to jump right in and completely butcher some Britney Spears and Christina Aguilera songs.

Alexander hasn't mentioned Melanie since our conversation last week. Of course, we've both been so busy we haven't seen that much of each other either. Once the party is over I'm going to have to sit down and talk to him. He needs to know about Melanie and Jake and their master plan to try to break us up.

"Awe. Everything looks so nice," Angie says loudly. "Not as great as my Halloween party but a close second."

I giggle. "Thanks. I'm glad I could make you proud."

I notice Brett standing behind her looking super pale. I can see how nervous he is already.

"I can't believe the last time we were all here together was Halloween," she says sadly. "A lot has happened since then."

I nod.

"Oh, I have to go say hi to Vinny. I'll be right back."

While Angie greets her cousin, who is also bartending for us, Brett pulls me outside on the deck.

"Are we all set?" he whispers loudly. "I'm freaking out. Do you think she's going to say yes?"

I start laughing.

"Of course. Relax."

He motions for me to follow him. Once we are a good distance away from the French doors, he takes a small box out of his pocket. I gasp when he opens it to show me the beautiful engagement ring.

I squeal in delight. "She's going to love it."

He relaxes a little. "You sure?"

"Yes."

"What are you two up to?" Angie asks.

Both Brett and I jump when we hear her voice. He shoves the box into his pocket.

We both turn around as she slowly wanders over to join us.

"We aren't up to anything," I reply. "I was just having a private talk with Brett, reminding him that he better take good care of you for me or else."

She gives us a skeptical look but doesn't question me. Whew. That was close.

"Welcome, everyone."

Alexander is standing in the doorway munching on chips and salsa.

"Look who it is," Angie says excitedly. She runs over to give him a hug, and Brett is right behind her to shake his hand.

"Since Summer just gave Brett a lecture about taking care of me, it's my turn."

She drags Alexander back inside the house. Brett gives me a grateful smile and follows them.

This is crazy; my best friend is about to get engaged. I could stand here and cry or I could go inside and get this party started. I watch Alexander talking to my friends, and he fits in so perfectly. He looks at me and gives me a wink, reminding me of how much I adore him.

The guests slowly trickle in, and it's a great turnout. Angie and Brett obviously have a lot of friends, so Brett's going to have quite the audience for his big proposal. The karaoke machine is a huge hit. Angie and Gina don't waste any time performing several songs. I even join them in singing "I Will Survive."

Alexander comes up behind me, wrapping his arms around my waist. "Having fun?"

I give him a kiss on the cheek. "Yes. I was just thinking that soon I wouldn't be seeing Angie every day or even every other day. It's just surreal."

Alexander nuzzles into my neck. "I understand. But you still have me."

Before I have a chance to respond, Brett interrupts us.

"I'm ready."

Suddenly, my adrenaline kicks in and I quietly call all the guests into the living room.

Angie and her cousin just finish a very poor rendition of "I Got You Babe," when Brett takes the microphone.

Here we go.

Alexander joins me and wraps his arm around me. Brett begins by thanking everyone for coming.

"Angie and I appreciate you all and the roles you've played in our lives. We hope we have a lot of visitors in Florida."

Angie nods in agreement.

"Before we get back to partying, I wanted to say one more thing." He turns to Angie and grabs both her hands.

"What the hell is happening?" Gina says in my ear.

I shrug my shoulders and give her a knowing look.

"Oh my gosh," she says, putting her hand to her mouth.

"Angie, I know this was a very difficult decision to leave our lives behind and start fresh. You've already made me happier than I could imagine."

His voice is trembling, and he's obviously terrified. He drops to one knee, and the guests gasp.

"There's only one more thing you could do to complete my life and that would be if you agree to marry me."

Angie is speechless, which I've never seen before. The room is so quiet you could hear a pin drop.

"Are you kidding? Of course I'll marry you," she yells.

The crowd erupts in cheers and applause. There are a few tears shed—some by me.

"That was great. Good for them," Alexander says, after the crowd begins to disperse.

"I wish them a lot of luck. Marriage can be hard, but it can be fantastic, too."

Of course, I know he's referring to his marriage to Helena.

"I'm so happy for them," I say excitedly.

"Me, too. I'm sure they'll have a long and successful marriage. Some people aren't meant to be married, but I have a feeling they're going to make it."

Well, that's interesting. Is he referring to himself and Helena or just himself? Of course, we've never talked about marriage at all. It's much too early in our relationship for that kind of a conversation, and we have other issues to work through before that.

"Summer, you knew about this and didn't tell me? You know I hate surprises," Angie squeals. I give her a big hug and congratulate her and Brett.

"Only for a few days," I say with a giggle. "I would never have been able to keep that to myself for that long. And you have to admit, this surprise was pretty great."

"Let's see the rock," Gina says, interrupting us. She studies Angie's left hand very carefully for several seconds. "Oh yeah, that's a good one."

"You're moving and engaged," I say excitedly. "It's an exciting time for you."

She pulls me into another tight hug. We both get a little choked up, but before we have a chance to talk about this emotional moment, she's approached by several of the other guests. I stand back and watch, and I couldn't be happier for her. Spring has certainly brought her a fresh new start.

As much as I love a good party, I really dislike the cleanup. Alexander, Gina, Vinny, Brett, and Angie all stay to help clean up. Of course, we save the karaoke machine for last.

"Do you see what's happening over there?" Angie whispers.

I look in the direction she's pointing and sure enough Gina and Vinny have their heads together and they seem to be in deep discussion.

My mouth drops open. "Whoa. I would have never thought of that."

Angie's face falls.

"I can't believe I'm not going to be here for all of this. You and Alexander are on your way to the next step, and now Gina and Vinny are flirting. I'm going to miss everything."

I grab her hand and remind her of the gorgeous bling on her finger.

"You're making a fresh start with the love of your life. Enjoy it."

She nods. "You will always be my best friend, Summer, no matter how far apart we are."

I give her a big hug. "Of course."

"And will you promise me that you will let yourself be happy with Alexander?" she says loudly.

I shush her, but luckily no one is around to hear us.

"I'm trying. Hopefully, we can get everything sorted out with this Melanie situation."

"It will all work out. I know it," she insists.

I wish I could be as sure as she is.

Chapter Thirteen

I open my eyes to the sun streaming in the window. For a second, I don't even know where I am. Suddenly, I remember that after the good-bye party it was so late I ended up staying at Alexander's.

After I get ready, I wander downstairs to find Alexander sitting on the deck. He's drinking coffee and working on his laptop.

"Good morning," he says cheerfully.

Hah! It's already almost noon. I never sleep this late.

"I'm sorry I slept so late. I guess I needed the rest."

He grabs my hand and pulls me down to kiss me.

"I'm sure you did. You worked hard on that party."

I pour myself a cup of coffee and stir in some sugar and cream.

"Are you working?" I ask, pointing at his laptop.

He rolls his eyes.

"Just following up on a few things. I'll be done soon, and then I'm all yours."

I hate to ruin another good day but I need to address the elephant in the room. I wish I had his ability to avoid it, but that's just not me.

"I was hoping we could talk."

He looks up from his laptop and gets a worried look on his face.

"Okay."

I try to swallow the lump in my throat.

"I met up with Jake a few days ago, and he told me a few things. First of all, I was right, he and Melanie are not seeing each other. They pretended to be together to try to make us jealous and ultimately break us up."

Alexander stares at me as if I'm speaking in another language.

"I know it's hard for you to believe that Melanie is capable of these things, but I assure you she is. Jake also told me that he was still in love with me and that Melanie is in love with you."

I wait for Alexander to say something . . . anything.

"Please say something."

"I'm so sorry," he says sadly.

Okay, that's something. But what's he apologizing for?

"I let this get out of hand. I appreciate Melanie for all her service over the years. I guess I never believed it would get to this level."

"Have you spoken to her since our conversation?" I ask.

He nods.

"She insisted that what happened in Pottery Barn was a misunderstanding. She actually told me she was happy with Jake and things were progressing for them."

"She was trying to make you jealous," I interrupt.

Really? A misunderstanding. What kind of hold does she have over him? I have to give her credit because she's a master manipulator.

"I've been so unfair to you, Summer. I promise I will take care of this once and for all. Can I ask just ask one more thing of you?"

I stare at his gorgeous face, and I can see the sincerity in his eyes. Suddenly, Angie's words play over in my head about letting myself be happy with him.

"Yes."

"Can you give me a little more time? This is going to be a huge change in my life."

I don't say anything.

He pulls his chair over to mine and puts his hands on mine.

"Do you trust my feelings for you?"

Ugh. Of course I do, but I don't know if that's enough.

"I trust that you love me, but I believed Jake loved me, too. I gave him almost two years of my life."

He shakes his head. "I'm not like Jake."

I look away to avoid his eye contact. "I feel so guilty about forcing you to make this choice."

He takes my chin in his hand and turns my head to look back at him.

"Don't feel guilty. I'm going to prove to you how committed I am to making this work."

He gently pulls me into his arms. I close my eyes as I breathe in his scent. I have to have faith in him and in us. I need to believe that I'm making the right decision for my future and for this season in my life.

"I have a feeling things are just going to get better from here."

I smile. "Me, too."

We spend the rest of the afternoon enjoying each other and this beautiful spring day.

THE END

Return to Summer Now Available

Buy the fourth book in the Seasons of Summer series on Amazon or read with your KindleUnlimited membership!

I'm fanning myself with my menu. Summer has arrived, and as much as I love it, I'm never prepared for the heat waves. As I look through my planner, I get excited. the next few months are going to be really busy, but I love it. It's been quite a year for me, and even as difficult as things got, I wouldn't change anything.

The most exciting thing happening is that after several months of searching, I found a new apartment. The plan is to move next month, assuming nothing else gets in the way. Unfortunately, little things seem to keep popping up that make me wonder if it's not a good idea to move, but I adore the place and the location is perfect.

The sound of my phone ringing distracts me from my thoughts of moving, and I smile when I see it's my best friend, Angie, calling.

"I finally get to talk to a real live person," I say sarcastically.

She giggles. "Me, too. I can't believe I haven't even been gone two months yet."

Angie recently moved to Florida. It was unexpected, so we're all still trying to get used to it (me especially).

"I know. It feels like an eternity since we've been able to talk."

Angie and I have been so busy, and other than texting, we haven't been able to catch up.

"Well, you're missing a brutal heat wave right now."

She starts to laugh. "You don't want to talk about a heat wave. It's ninety-eight degrees right now, and the only break we will get is when the afternoon thunderstorms roll in."

I have to admit that sounds miserable, but I know when winter comes I will be wishing I was there with her.

"What are you up to?" she asks.

"I'm waiting on Helena . . . again."

Helena is one of my clients. I, well, my company, Summer Interiors, has been redecorating her apartment. She also happens to be my boyfriend's ex-wife, but that's another story. Thankfully, I was able to remove the shrine she had up in her living room of their life together. I admit I used some serious reverse psychology, and for some reason, she fell for it.

"How's that going?" Angie asks.

"Surprisingly well. She's been much easier to work with than I expected."

This is true. I struggled with the decision of working with her, especially after one of her and Alexander's best friends told me they were soul mates and would get back together eventually. We had a few obstacles, but she's actually been one of my easier clients.

"That's good. And how's Alexander?"

I smile to myself. I feel like a giddy teenager when I think about him. We've been together since October, and despite some rocky times, things are really good right now.

"He's great."

"And Melanie?"

I sigh. Melanie (Alexander's assistant) would be the one area of our relationship that isn't great.

"She's still here," I say through gritted teeth.

"How can that be? After everything."

I continue to fan myself and take a sip of my water.

"Because she begged him to let her stay. She swore she would never meddle in our lives again and this was the best job she ever had. She laid it on thick, tears and all, and he fell for it. But, I have to admit she's stuck to her word . . . so far anyway."

She groans. "Well, keep your eye on her."

I snort. "Oh, trust me, Melanie is not going to make any more trouble for us."

I'm so involved in my conversation that I don't notice Helena has finally arrived.

"Oh dear, I wouldn't be so sure of that," Helena says adamantly. "Melanie is toxic, and you need to be careful."

I quickly get off the phone while Helena sits down. I'm not surprised by her reaction to Melanie, there's no love lost between them.

"I was just talking to my best friend, and she asked me about Melanie. I know there's a lot of bad blood between you."

She folds her arms.

"You don't know the full story, do you?"

I give her a curious look. "About you and Melanie?"

She raises her eyebrows. "I think it's about time for you to hear what really happened with my marriage to Xander.

Then, you'll fully understand who Melanie is and who you're dealing with."

Dear Reader

I hope you enjoyed *To Spring with Love: A Novella*. Please take a few minutes to leave a review on Amazon.

Love my books? Join my Facebook reader group. Interested in a free book? Click here.

Visit my website for updates, and stay tuned for my next book coming soon.

authormelissabaldwin.com

Also by Melissa Baldwin

COZY MYSTERY

Killer Couture: A Small-Town Cozy Mystery

Poison in Paradise: a tropical romantic mystery

Movie Scripts & Madness (The Madness and Murder Mysteries #1)

Room Service & Murder (The Madness and Murder Mysteries #2)

ROMANTIC COMEDY

Can't Hurry Christmas: A Holiday Romantic Comedy

Now That We Don't Talk: A Romantic Comedy

All the Christmas Vibes: A Holiday Romantic Comedy

Love in Overtime: A Sweet Small Town Hockey Romcom (Love on Thin Ice Multi-Author Series)

Soulmates and Slapshots: A Sweet Small Town Hockey Romcom (Love in Maple Falls Multi-Author Series)

Can We Talk?: A Romantic Comedy (Question #1)

I Think He Knows?: A Romantic Comedy (Question #2)

A Very Complicated Christmas: A Holiday Romantic Comedy

Unlucky Christmas: A Holiday Romantic Comedy

It Could Happen: A Romantic Comedy

Friends ForNever: A Romantic Comedy

One Way Ticket (written with Kate O'Keeffe)

Thanks for the Love: A Novella (Thankful #1)

Thanks for the Memories (Thankful #2)

Thanks for the Friendship (Thankful #3)

Love and Ohana Drama (Twist of Fate #1

Fate and Blind Dates (Twist of Fate #2)

Glances and Taking Chances (Twist of Fate #3)

On the Road to Love (Love in the City #1)

All You Need is Love (Love in the City #2)

From Runway to Love (Love in the City #3)

Fall Into Magic (Seasons of Summer #1)

Winter Can Wait (Seasons of Summer #2)

To Spring With Love (Seasons of Summer #3)

Return to Summer (Seasons of Summer #4)

See You Soon Broadway (Broadway #1)

See You Later Broadway (Broadway #2)

An Event to Remember (Event to Remember #1)

Wedding Haters (Event to Remember #2)

Not Quite Sheer Happiness (Event to Remember #3)

About the Author

USA Today bestselling author Melissa Baldwin always dreamed of sharing her stories with the world. She brought this vision to life, becoming an award-winning, bestselling author of over thirty romantic comedies and cozy mysteries. Melissa is also a wife, mother, new empty-nester, and travel advisor.

Her books feature charming, ambitious, and real women, whom she considers part of her tribe. Although she rarely takes a day off, when she's not writing, she enjoys quality time with her family, traveling, attempting yoga poses, and booking Disney vacations. Melissa still uses a paper planner, and her guilty pleasures include Beverly Hills 90210 reruns and General Hospital.